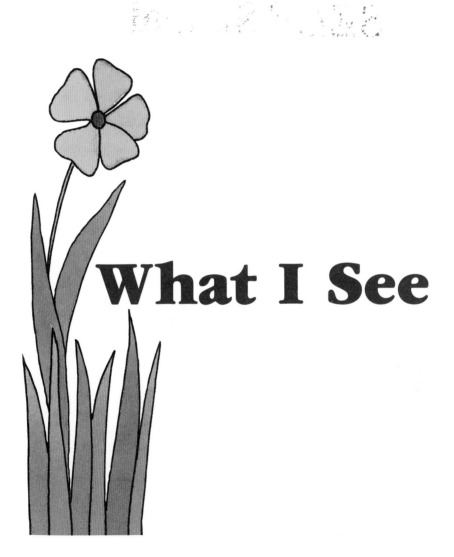

What I See

What I

Holly Keller

Green Light Readers
Harcourt Brace & Company
San Diego   New York   London

See

Requests for permission to make copies of any part of the work should be mailed to:
Permissions Department, Harcourt Brace & Company, 6277 Sea Harbor Drive,
Orlando, Florida 32887-6777.

First Green Light Readers edition 1999
Green Light Readers is a trademark of Harcourt Brace & Company.

The Library of Congress has cataloged the original paperback edition as follows:
Keller, Holly.
What I see/Holly Keller.
p.   cm.
"Green Light Readers."
Summary: Illustrations and simple rhyming text describe what
a child sees around the house and garden.
ISBN 0-15-202393-3
ISBN 0-15-201996-0 (pb)
[1. Stories in rhyme.]   I. Title.
PZ8.3.K275Wh   1999
[E]—dc21   98-17519

A C E F D B

B D F G E C (pb)

Printed in Mexico.

I see a rose.

I see a nose.

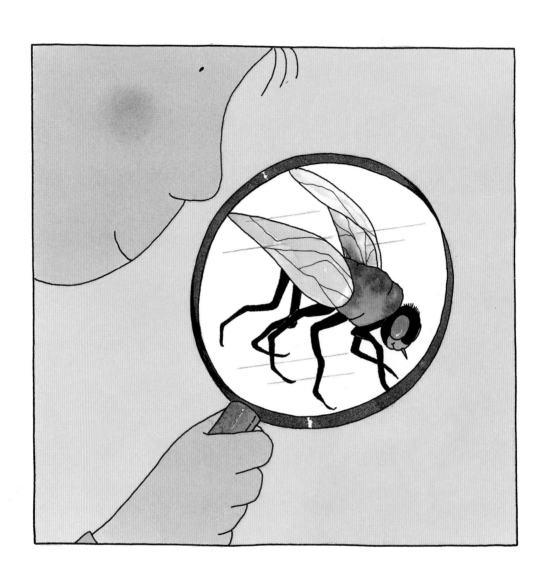

I see a fly.

I see a pie.

I see a cat.

I see a mat.

I see a top.

I see a mop.

I see a dog.

I see a frog.

I see a bee.

I see me!

The illustrations in this book were done in black pen, watercolor,
and pastel on Rives BFK paper.
The display type was set in Garamond Ultra.
The text type was set in Minion.
Color separations by Bright Arts Ltd., Hong Kong
This book was printed on 140-gsm matte art paper.
Production supervision by Stanley Redfern and Ginger Boyer
Designed by Barry Age